HOPSCOTCH

Marlowe's Mum and the Tree House

First published in 2004 by
Franklin Watts
338 Euston Road
London
NW1 3BH

Franklin Watts Australia
Level 17 / 207 Kent Street
Sydney
NSW 2000

A CIP catalogue record for this book is available
from the British Library.

ISBN 978 0 7496 5874 8

Series Editor: Jackie Hamley
Series Advisor: Dr Barrie Wade
Cover Design: Jason Anscomb
Design: Peter Scoulding

Printed in China

Franklin Watts is a division of
Hachette Children's Books.

For James and Nathaniel – K.L.

HOPSCOTCH

Marlowe's Mum and the Tree House

by Karina Law and Ross Collins

W
FRANKLIN WATTS
LONDON•SYDNEY

"Right! That's it!" said Marlowe's
mum. "I'm getting out of here!"

"Where are you going?" asked Marlowe. Mum sounded cross. "To the tree house. Maybe I'll get some peace up there," she said.

"But it's teatime!" said Marlowe.

"Tell your dad," replied Mum.

"I've had enough."

"Dad," said Marlowe,
"Mum's left home."

"Yes, Marlowe.

In a minute," said Dad.

"DAD," said Marlowe, a little louder. "MUM'S LEFT HOME!"

"LEFT HOME?" said Dad.

"What do you mean, *left home*?"

"She's gone to my tree house,"
said Marlowe. Dad looked worried.
"Perhaps she's not well," he said.

Dad called Doctor Frost.
"She's a bit under the weather,"
reported Doctor Frost. "Leave
her for a day or two and I'm
sure she'll be as right as rain."

Mrs Jones, from next door,
popped round for a chat. Mum
didn't seem to want to chat.

Dad left a tray of tea and
cakes for Mum. But Mum
didn't come down.

Mum was still up in the tree
house at bedtime. Dad had to
do *everything*.

Mum was still up in the tree house
the next morning. But the tray
had gone and there
was a note.

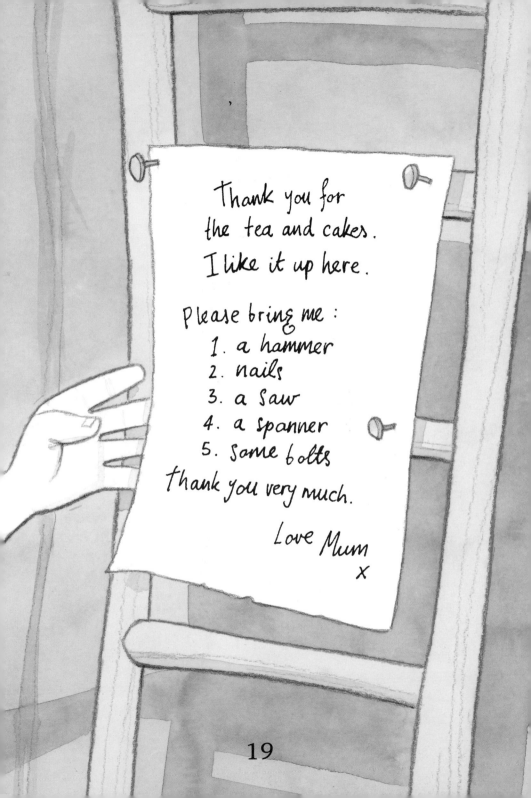

"Nails?" said Dad with surprise.

"A hammer?" said Marlowe.

Marlowe and Dad fetched the

things Mum wanted.

They left them at the foot of the ladder. "Perhaps Mum's going to fix the leak in the roof of the tree house," suggested Dad.

Everyone
missed Mum.

The next day, Mum was still in the tree house. There was a new note.

Please bring me :
1. a mop
2. a duster
3. soap
4. a skateboard

Thank you very much.
Love
Mum x

24

There were some very strange
noises coming from the tree house.

Marlowe and Dad fetched the things Mum wanted and left them at the foot of the ladder. "Perhaps Mum wants to do some cleaning," said Marlowe. "On wheels?" asked Dad, shaking his head.

Mum stayed up in the tree house
for three whole days. On the fourth
day, at teatime, Mum came home.

Everyone was so pleased to see her.
Mum gave them all lots of hugs
and kisses. But Mum wasn't alone!

Hopscotch has been specially designed to fit the requirements of the National Literacy Strategy. It offers real books by top authors and illustrators for children developing their reading skills. There are 49 Hopscotch stories to choose from:

Marvin, the Blue Pig
ISBN 978 0 7496 4619 6

Plip and Plop
ISBN 978 0 7496 4620 2

The Queen's Dragon
ISBN 978 0 7496 4618 9

Flora McQuack
ISBN 978 0 7496 4621 9

Willie the Whale
ISBN 978 0 7496 4623 3

Naughty Nancy
ISBN 978 0 7496 4622 6

Run!
ISBN 978 0 7496 4705 6

The Playground Snake
ISBN 978 0 7496 4706 3

"Sausages!"
ISBN 978 0 7496 4707 0

Bear in Town
ISBN 978 0 7496 5875 5

Pippin's Big Jump
ISBN 978 0 7496 4710 0

Whose Birthday Is It?
ISBN 978 0 7496 4709 4

The Princess and the Frog
ISBN 978 0 7496 5129 9

Flynn Flies High
ISBN 978 0 7496 5130 5

Clever Cat
ISBN 978 0 7496 5131 2

Moo!
ISBN 978 0 7496 5332 3

Izzie's Idea
ISBN 978 0 7496 5334 7

Roly-poly Rice Ball
ISBN 978 0 7496 5333 0

I Can't Stand It!
ISBN 978 0 7496 5765 9

Cockerel's Big Egg
ISBN 978 0 7496 5767 3

How to Teach a Dragon Manners
ISBN 978 0 7496 5873 1

The Truth about those Billy Goats
ISBN 978 0 7496 5766 6

Marlowe's Mum and the Tree House
ISBN 978 0 7496 5874 8

The Truth about Hansel and Gretel
ISBN 978 0 7496 4708 7

The Best Den Ever
ISBN 978 0 7496 5876 2

ADVENTURE STORIES

Aladdin and the Lamp
ISBN 978 0 7496 6692 7

Blackbeard the Pirate
ISBN 978 0 7496 6690 3

George and the Dragon
ISBN 978 0 7496 6691 0

Jack the Giant-Killer
ISBN 978 0 7496 6693 4

TALES OF KING ARTHUR

1. The Sword in the Stone
ISBN 978 0 7496 6694 1

2. Arthur the King
ISBN 978 0 7496 6695 8

3. The Round Table
ISBN 978 0 7496 6697 2

4. Sir Lancelot and the Ice Castle
ISBN 978 0 7496 6698 9

TALES OF ROBIN HOOD

Robin and the Knight
ISBN 978 0 7496 6699 6

Robin and the Monk
ISBN 978 0 7496 6700 9

Robin and the Silver Arrow
ISBN 978 0 7496 6703 0

Robin and the Friar
ISBN 978 0 7496 6702 3

FAIRY TALES

The Emperor's New Clothes
ISBN 978 0 7496 7421 2

Cinderella
ISBN 978 0 7496 7417 5

Snow White
ISBN 978 0 7496 7418 2

Jack and the Beanstalk
ISBN 978 0 7496 7422 9

The Three Billy Goats Gruff
ISBN 978 0 7496 7420 5

The Pied Piper of Hamelin
ISBN 978 0 7496 7419 9

HISTORIES

Toby and the Great Fire of London
ISBN 978 0 7496 7079 5 *
ISBN 978 0 7496 7410 6

Pocahontas the Peacemaker
ISBN 978 0 7496 7080 1 *
ISBN 978 0 7496 7411 3

Grandma's Seaside Bloomers
ISBN 978 0 7496 7081 8 *
ISBN 978 0 7496 7412 0

Hoorah for Mary Seacole
ISBN 978 0 7496 7082 5 *
ISBN 978 0 7496 7413 7

Remember the 5th of November
ISBN 978 0 7496 7083 2 *
ISBN 978 0 7496 7414 4

Tutankhamun and the Golden Chariot
ISBN 978 0 7496 7084 9 *
ISBN 978 0 7496 7415 1

* hardback